This book belongs to:

_____

_____

_____

To Lili, my little clown
To Séverine

• Little, Brown and Company • Hachette Book Group • 1290 Avenue of the Americas, New York, NY 10104 • Visit us at LBYR.com • Originally published by Hachette Enfants/Hachette Livre in France as *Les émotions de Gaston—Je suis timide* © Hachette Livre / Hachette Enfants. 2018 • First U.S. Edition: January 2020 • Little, Brown and Company is a division of Hachette Book Group, Inc. • The Little, Brown name and logo are trademarks of Hachette Book Group, Inc. • The publisher is not responsible for websites (or their content) that are not owned by the publisher. • Library of Congress Cataloging-in-Publication Data • Names: Chien Chow Chine, Aurélie, author, illustrator. • Title: Little Unicorn is shy / Aurélie Chien Chow Chine. • Other titles: Les émotions de Gaston - Je suis timide. English • Description: First U.S. edition. | New York : Little, Brown and Company, 2020. | Originally published in France by Hachette Enfants/Hachette Livre in 2018 under title: Les émotions de Gaston - Je suis timide. | Summary: A little unicorn feels all kinds of emotions, including shyness, and uses a breathing exercise to calm down. • Identifiers: LCCN 2018060502| ISBN 9780316532105 (hardcover) | ISBN 9780316531948 (ebook) | ISBN 9780316532099 (library edition ebook) • Subjects: | CYAC: Bashfulness—Fiction. | Breathing exercises—Fiction. | Unicorns—Fiction. • Classification: LCC PZ7.1.C4978 Lm 2020 | DDC [E]—dc23 • LC record available at https://lccn.loc.gov/2018060502 • ISBNs: 978-0-316-53210-5 (hardcover), 978-0-316-53197-9 (ebook), 978-0-316-53194-8 (ebook), 978-0-316-53195-5 (ebook) • PRINTED IN CHINA • APS • 10 9 8 7 6 5 4 3 2 1

Little Unicorn IS SHY

Aurélie Chien Chow Chine

LITTLE, BROWN AND COMPANY
NEW YORK   BOSTON

This is Little Unicorn.
He is very much like all the other little unicorns....

Sometimes, **Little Unicorn** is okay.
Sometimes, he is **not** okay.
Sometimes, he is angry.
Sometimes, he is happy.
Sometimes, he is shy.

These are emotions.

And **Little Unicorn** feels all kinds of emotions.
Just like you.

But there is something that makes **Little Unicorn** special:
He has a **magical mane**!

When all is well, his mane shines
with the colors of the rainbow.

But when all isn't well, his mane changes...
and its color shows just what he feels.

Happy

Jealous

Angry

Guilty

Shy

Scared

Stubborn

Sad

How does **Little Unicorn** feel right now?

Pretty good...

But his heart feels a little sunny and cloudy
at the same time, and he's going to tell us why.

And you, how do you feel today?

Great   Good   Fine

Not good   Bad   Awful

Now, why doesn't **Little Unicorn** feel perfect?

Most of the time, **Little Unicorn** is full
of fun and loves acting like a clown with
his family and friends.

But there are moments when **Little Unicorn**
doesn't feel that comfortable.

Today is his birthday. When the mail carrier
brings him his mail, **Little Unicorn**
hides behind Mama.

At school, his teacher and classmates sing,
"Happy birthday, Little Unicorn!"

He doesn't feel comfortable with everyone
looking at him. He enjoys the song,
but he doesn't know how to react.
Little Unicorn is embarrassed.

After school, Mama and **Little Unicorn** go
to the bakery to buy a birthday cake.
The kind baker offers him a lollipop.

Little Unicorn loves lollipops,
but he doesn't dare take it. He is **shy**.

That afternoon, his family and friends come over
to celebrate his birthday. They stand around
the cake and sing to him.

But **Little Unicorn** doesn't enjoy the moment.
He feels different emotions at the same time.
He's happy to be with his family and friends,
but he doesn't like being the center of attention.

He wishes he could be as small as a mouse.

Little Unicorn covers his eyes,
as if that could make him disappear.

What if, instead of feeling as small as a mouse,
he could feel as big as a tiger to overcome his shyness?

ROAAR

He can!

And when you feel timid, you too can
imagine yourself as a tiger and do this
breathing exercise to overcome shyness.

Breathing exercise
to overcome your shyness

1. **Little Unicorn** closes his eyes. He imagines a handsome tiger costume. He breathes in through his nose, inflating his belly, and raises his arms in front of him.

2. **Little Unicorn** holds his breath. He grabs his imaginary costume with strong claws and puts it on.

3 With the **power** of a tiger,
   Little Unicorn blows the air out of his
   mouth and relaxes his shoulders and hands.

4 **Little Unicorn** begins to feel stronger
because of his tiger costume.

Little Unicorn does this exercise **three times.**

It takes at least **three breaths**
to transform into a true tiger!

Then he begins to breathe normally.
Now that he's put on his magnificent tiger costume,
he feels **confident,**
and the **beautiful sun** can shine in.

Ah, **Little Unicorn** is much more comfortable.
His good mood is back, and
the rainbow has returned to his mane.
He'll be able to fully enjoy the rest of his birthday.

If you overcome your shyness with your
tiger costume and powerful breathing, you can
enjoy every moment and feel at **peace**.
And your *smile* will return!

Don't miss these other stories about
Little Unicorn!

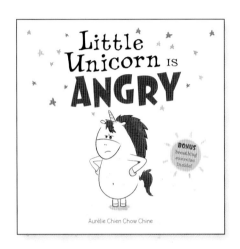

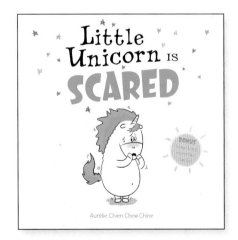
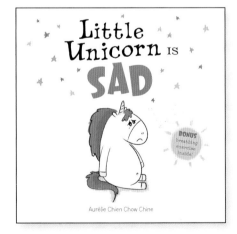

Available now!